With special thanks to Stephen Cole

To Matthew Egerton

www.beastquest.co.uk

ORCHARD BOOKS
338 Euston Road, London NW1 3BH
Orchard Books Australia
Level 17/207 Kent St, Sydney, NSW 2000

A Paperback Original
First published in Great Britain in 2007

Beast Quest is a registered trademark of Working Partners Limited
Series created by Working Partners Limited, London

Text © Working Partners Limited 2007
Cover illustration © David Wyatt 2007
Inside illustrations © Orchard Books 2007

A CIP catalogue record for this book is available
from the British Library.

ISBN 978 1 84616 487 3

16

Printed in Great Britain

The paper and board used in this paperback are natural recyclable
products made from wood grown in sustainable forests. The
manufacturing processes conform to the environmental regulations
of the country of origin.

Orchard Books is a division of Hachette Children's Books,
an Hachette UK company.

www.hachette.co.uk

EPOS
THE FLAME BIRD

BY ADAM BLADE

ORCHARD BOOKS

THE ICY

THE NORTHERN
MOUNTAINS

THE

WESTERN OCEAN

THE FOREST
OF FEAR

TH

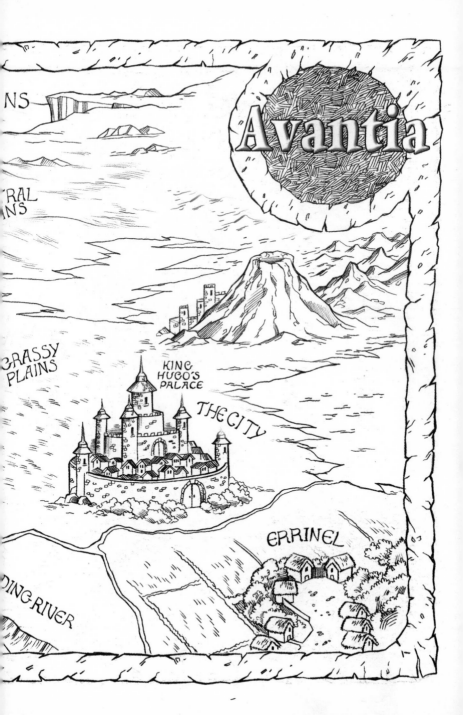

Welcome to the kingdom of Avantia. I am Aduro – a good wizard residing in the palace of King Hugo. You join us at a difficult time. Let me explain...

It is written in the Ancient Scripts that our peaceful kingdom shall one day be plunged into peril.

Now that time has come.

Under the evil spell of Malvel the Dark Wizard, six Beasts – fire dragon, sea serpent, mountain giant, horse-man, snow monster and flame bird – run wild and destroy the land they once protected.

Avantia is in great danger.

The Ancient Scripts also predict an unlikely hero. It is written that a boy shall take up the Quest to free the Beasts from the curse and save the kingdom.

We do not know who this boy is, only that his time has come...

We pray our young hero will have the courage and the heart to take up the Quest. Will you join us as we wait and watch?

Avantia salutes you,

Aduro

PROLOGUE

"I'm lost," thought Owen.

The tunnel ended in yet another dark cave. Panic rose in the boy's throat as he tried to re-trace his steps. But he knew it was hopeless. Although he had left chalk markings on the rock walls, it was too dark to see them.

Only a while ago, Owen had been playing outside the caves on the north side of the village. Then he had heard noises coming from inside the caves. Scraping, scrabbling noises. People hardly ever entered the caves, as they were unsafe and stretched for miles underground. Rockfalls were common, too. But he couldn't just ignore whatever was in there.

"An animal must have wandered in and got lost," he'd told himself. "It won't take long to help the poor thing back out."

He had tried to follow the scrabbling sounds he had heard – and now he was hopelessly lost. He stood helpless in the cold blackness.

"Is anyone there?" he called. His voice echoed eerily back at him. These caves took the slightest sound and twisted it, making it seem as though it came from one direction when it came from another.

He felt ahead and his fingers brushed against pitted rock – then nothing.

Stepping forwards, Owen realised he'd found the mouth of a new cave.

A little way in, there was a faint light. He looked up and saw a chink of grey sky in the rock, high above.

Then his foot scraped against something on the floor. It was a piece of scorched armour. Where had this come from? And what had happened to the knight who had worn it? It looked like a bevor – which knights used to protect the chin and lower face – only smaller.

Suddenly a terrifying screech sliced through the air. Owen yelled out in terror, staring round wildly.

A dark shape detached itself from the shadows and towered over him. In horror Owen saw it was a giant bird!

Its huge, sail-like wings unfurled. They were covered in short, dark-gold feathers. Its beak was as long

and sharp as a sword. Two fierce eyes
fixed on Owen, blazing like irons in
a blacksmith's fire. The creature's
huge talons were scratching on the
rock, tearing it up. Heart pounding,
Owen realised that this was the
sound he had heard. Here was the
animal he had hoped to rescue...
Now *he* needed rescuing – and fast!

The creature lurched towards him –
and then its massive, feathered bulk
burst into flame! Owen hurled
himself to the ground as the Beast
launched into the air, its great fiery
wings beating wildly as it flew
straight at him...

CHAPTER ONE

THE FIERY THREAT

"We must be nearly through the forest now," Tom called to his friend Elenna, who was walking behind him. He drew his sword and hacked at the thorny thicket barring his way. The light was thin, the grey sky barely visible through the heavy branches overhead.

"Don't worry – I'll make it," Elenna assured him. She was leading Storm,

Tom's sturdy black stallion, and stopped for a moment, leaning against the horse for support. "But a rest would be good."

Her pet wolf, Silver, sank into the long grass beside her and barked.

"Hear that?" Elenna smiled. "Silver agrees with me."

But Tom shook his head. "It has taken us almost two weeks to get this far. We must keep going."

"Not many people would be in such a rush to battle a giant flame bird!" said Elenna.

Tom was exhausted, too. But with a swell of determination, he raised his blade and swiped fiercely at the undergrowth. He was on a vital quest for King Hugo of Avantia. He couldn't give up now the end was almost in sight.

His mission was to save the

kingdom from the menace of the Beasts – creatures of legend placed under an evil spell by the Dark Wizard, Malvel. Tom used to think the Beasts were just fairy stories. But now he knew there was nothing make-believe about them.

Elenna and Silver had joined Tom and Storm on the Quest, and together they had risked their lives trying to set the Beasts free from Malvel's curse. They had already faced up to a one-eyed giant and a slithering sea serpent. They had tackled a horse-man, a fire dragon and a terrifying snow monster. Now their task was to free Epos the flame bird from the dark enchantment she was under.

Tom pulled his shield from his back and used it to crush some bracken. "Let's rest for a few minutes while we check the map," he said to Elenna.

"Great!" said Elenna, slumping to the ground beside Silver.

Storm leaned over and rested his muzzle on her shoulder, snorting softly.

Tom reached into his pocket to pull out the magical map of Avantia. It had been given to them by the king's closest adviser – Wizard Aduro.

Tom sat beside Elenna. As his finger traced over the trees, hills and lakes, the pictures rose up from the parchment, standing as tall as his thumbnail. A pulsing green line marked the path he and Elenna had taken from the ice fields of the far north to this great forest of the east.

"We're nearly at the forest's edge," said Tom, with relief.

Elenna pointed to a miniature mountain on the map, just beyond the forest. "That must be a volcano."

As she watched, tiny puffs of smoke seemed to rise up from the mountain.

"It's supposed to be dormant," said Tom. "Well, according to the map, that's where we'll find Epos." A thrill of anticipation ran through him. "Aduro said she was the most powerful of all the Beasts."

He frowned at the map. "Why would anyone build a village that close to a volcano – even a dormant one?"

"The soil around volcanoes is very fertile, so crops grow well," said Elenna. "I learned that from my uncle." She looked down at her hands. "It's been so long since I left my village. I miss the people there."

Tom smiled. "When we finish our Quest, I bet Aduro will take you home."

"But what about you?" said Elenna. "Will you go back to your aunt and uncle in Errinel?"

"I expect so," said Tom, looking away. "But what I really want to do is find my father."

Tom's mother had died when he was born, and his father, Taladon, had disappeared soon afterwards. Tom had been raised by his aunt and uncle – but he still hoped to find his father some day. All he knew was that Taladon had served King Hugo in the past, just as Tom was doing now...

"Wait." Tom's nose twitched. "Can you smell...smoke?"

Elenna coughed. "Someone must have lit a fire."

Suddenly a loud rumble sounded through the forest, and the ground beneath them shook. Storm neighed and reared up in alarm, as Tom and Elenna scrambled to their feet. Tom looked up. Through the leaves he

glimpsed clouds of dark smoke
choking the sky. They were shot
through with thin streaks of fire like
shooting stars.

"The volcano," Elenna gasped. "It's
going to erupt!"

"We need to find shelter," Tom
said. "That flame bird must be
stirring things up!"

Then Elenna froze. "Look," she
stammered, staring straight past Tom.

Whirling round, Tom felt his heart

leap into his throat. A huge bird-like creature stood in a small clearing not far away from them. It had a sharp, jutting beak, and violet flames flickered and sparked all around it. A golden band was attached to one of its muscular legs, and the earth smoked beneath its talons. Its massive, glittering wings brushed against the nearby bushes – and set them alight.

"Epos," Tom breathed, his fingers

tightening round his sword hilt. "We came here to find her – but she's found us!"

The Beast's fierce red eyes narrowed as it rose into the blazing forest. Tom saw a fireball forming from the violet flames at its feet.

Then, with a shriek of rage, Epos hurled the ball of flame – straight at Tom!

CHAPTER TWO

BURNING SECRETS

"Get back!" Tom shouted, throwing up his shield in front of him.

Elenna frantically pushed Storm into the tangled trees, Silver snapping at her heels.

The fireball hit the shield and exploded. Tom gasped as hundreds of tiny violet embers flew through the air and set light to everything they touched. Willing himself to stay calm, he turned back to his friend.

"Take Storm," he yelled. "Ride as fast as you can to the village by the volcano and fetch help."

Elenna jumped onto the horse's back, choking on thick black smoke. "Be careful, Tom!" she cried. Then she pressed her heels to Storm's ribs and the stallion plunged forwards, with Silver close behind.

Tom whirled back to face Epos. With a thrill of terror he saw the Beast was forming a fresh fireball between its talons.

It took all Tom's courage, but he stood his ground and raised his wooden shield. At the bottom of the shield was a gleaming scale that had belonged to Ferno the fire dragon. It gave protection against fire – but could it stand up to a second blast of Epos's enchanted flames?

The fireball smashed into the shield with such force that Tom was knocked to the ground. The shield smouldered, but it didn't crack.

The flame bird squawked angrily, then crashed up through the blazing canopy of leaves and flew off into the grey sky.

"Come back here!" Tom shouted, his eyes streaming with smoke. "I'm not finished with you yet!"

But now he was surrounded by flames. The Beast's fireball had set fire to all the trees around him. "What shall I do?" he asked himself, suddenly panic-stricken.

As he looked desperately for a way out, Tom caught a glimpse of something rushing towards him.

It was a group of masked men!

Before he could react he was grabbed by his wrists and ankles, and lifted from the ground...

"Hey!" Tom yelled. "Let me go!"

"There's gratitude for you," puffed the man holding Tom's wrists.

"Anyone would think you didn't want to be helped!"

"Your friend sent us to fetch you. She's waiting for you at the village," explained another who was gripping his ankles.

Tom felt a dizzying wave of relief, and, after a few minutes, the men lowered him to the ground. They had escaped the worst of the flames.

Tom stood up and brushed himself down. "Thanks! I'm Tom, by the way."

"I'm Raymond," the first man said. "We'll have to leave you here for the moment. The village is completely cut off by the forest fire. If we don't fight it, our homes will burn to the ground. And with the volcano ready to blow, too… Things are looking bad. But we have to do something!"

Then the thick curtain of smoke parted, and Tom realised they were at the village near the foot of the volcano. The forest fire had almost reached the first houses, and a group of villagers was trying to stop it. He watched Raymond and the other man sprint back to help.

Then he felt something lick his hand. It was Silver!

Elenna followed with a pitcher of water. "Oh, Tom," she said. "I'm so glad you're all right!" As he gratefully gulped down the water, she lowered her voice. "What happened to Epos?"

"She flew away," said Tom, still panting for breath, as Storm leaned forward to nuzzle his hair.

"We've met six Beasts now," said Elenna, "and none of them came looking for a fight – except this one."

"I know," Tom said, watching as the villagers ran back and forth, desperately trying to control the forest fire. "Something tells me that Epos really means business. She's made sure the village is surrounded by fire. Now no one can get in – or out."

Elenna nodded. "Did you see that golden band round her leg?"

"That must be how Malvel is controlling her," Tom agreed. "We need to remove it – and fast."

Just then a skinny, fair-haired boy of about Tom's age burst out of the blazing forest, coughing hard, a singed sack in one hand – he must have been trying to beat the fire out. A piece of old armour protected his chin and neck. He flopped down on the grass.

Elenna and Tom ran over to him.

"Are you all right?" Tom asked the boy, helping him to take off the armour round his neck. "What's your name?"

"Owen," he croaked, staring up at

them. Soot covered his face. "Our village is going to be destroyed! There are too few of us to stop the fires."

Elenna gave him the pitcher of water, and the boy drank thirstily.

"Where's everyone else?" Tom asked, but he was looking closely at the piece of armour in his hands.

"Most people left when the volcano first stirred," said Owen weakly. "My family and a few others stayed to try and protect the crops. We didn't realise how bad things were going to get."

Elenna looked towards the smoking volcano. "And now we're all trapped."

"Never mind that," Tom said. He grabbed Owen by the shoulder. "Where did you get this armour?"

Owen frowned. "I...I found it in the caves."

"Where's the rest of it?" Tom demanded. He tried to keep his feelings under control, but he could feel his fingers tighten on the boy's shoulder.

"I don't know!" Owen wailed, pulling away. He jumped to his feet and scowled at Tom, rubbing his shoulder.

"Tom!" Elenna dragged his hand away. "What's got into you?"

"Sorry," he murmured. "But you see...this armour was made at the forge where I grew up." He pointed to a small hammer design stamped into the metal. "My uncle stamped his hallmark on everything he sold."

Elenna took the armour and studied it. "Hey, there's something else scratched here." She rubbed soot and rust away from the plate's metal rim and read, "T...A...L...A..."

"Taladon," whispered Tom, his stomach fizzing with excitement.

"Elenna – this armour belonged to my father!"

CHAPTER THREE

ESCAPE TO THE CAVES

Tom tried on the piece of armour. It fitted perfectly.

Elenna stared at him. "That means your father had his own armour when he was a boy. Why?"

"I don't know," Tom admitted. "My father wasn't a knight," he said, taking the piece of armour off and looking at it thoughtfully.

Suddenly the ground beneath them shook again and plumes of crimson fire streaked across the sky.

"The volcano!" Owen gasped.

Elenna clutched at her throat. Tom felt it, too. The air was suddenly much hotter. It stung their skin, and each breath burned their lungs.

"Take cover!" roared Raymond, stumbling out of the blazing forest with another man in his arms.

Tom and Elenna helped Owen to the shelter of a large oak. Storm stood protectively over him, as pumice stone and soot showered down from above. Silver raced around the clearing, helping Raymond shepherd the exhausted villagers to shelter.

They all waited tensely as the vibrations in the ground slowly came to a stop.

Raymond wiped soot and sweat from his face. "We can't stop the fire," he panted. "And if the volcano erupts we won't stand a chance out in the open. We'll have to shelter in the caves and hope for a miracle."

Elenna looked at Tom. "I wonder if we'll find the rest of that armour?"

Tom's heart thudded in his chest. All his life he had been desperate to know more about his father. Now he had found a clue – at the worst possible time. He shook his head. "The Quest comes first."

Raymond pulled a horn from his pocket. "I'll sound the emergency signal. Everyone in the village knows to gather at the caves when they hear it."

Elenna frowned. "But if the volcano does erupt, the caves might fill with lava!"

"There's nowhere else we can go," said a woman.

"Wait a moment," said Tom, reaching for the magical map of Avantia that he kept in his pocket. He unrolled it and looked closely at the caves. A faint red line threaded through them – a path! He rolled up the map again quickly before anyone could see. "I think there's a way through the caves to safety," he announced. "It comes out not far from the royal city."

"It's possible." Raymond nodded slowly.

"Perhaps we can ask the king for help," said Owen, his face lighting up.

"It's our only chance," said Tom.

Raymond nodded, then blew into the horn, a low, booming note that Tom guessed would carry for miles.

Tom and Elenna followed Raymond

as he led the way through the ruined village. Storm carried Owen and a wounded woman on his back. Sharp pumice and thick soot coated the roads and buildings. A foul stink of rotten eggs hung in the smoky air. Tom guessed the smell came from the sulphur that had been spewed up from the volcano's heart. People trudged along in silence. Silver looked all around as he walked, eyes bright and alert, ready to warn them of the tiniest tremble in the ground.

The rest of the villagers had already reached the caves by the time Raymond and Tom's party arrived. There were several men and women, and they were pale, dirty and exhausted. Three grimy dogs lay panting at their feet, and Silver trotted over to greet them. An older woman was snapping candles into three, ready to light their way. She gave a piece of candle each to Tom and Elenna with a smile.

Tom stared up into the dark mouth of the cave. Once, long ago, his father must have explored these caves. But had Taladon also encountered Epos?

"I'll lead the way," he said, turning to Raymond. "I've got a map, and I'm more rested than you. I can scout out the tunnels, check that we can all get through with the animals."

Raymond smiled. "You have spirit, Tom. Lead on."

As Tom stepped into the cave the cold air soothed his smarting skin. It was a relief to breathe cooler air. But the deeper they went, the more stale the air became.

The clatter of everyone's footsteps filled Tom's ears. Elenna walked behind him, leading Owen by the

hand, calling out words of
encouragement to all those following.
When Tom looked round he could
see the villagers clutching their
candles, each in their own pool of
weak light. They looked like ghosts in
the inky blackness. Rumbles from the
volcano made small streams of dust

pour down from the dark ceiling. The dogs began to whine, but Silver gave a stern bark and they fell silent. The wounded woman stirred on Storm's back, half-asleep with exhaustion, as the stallion stepped cautiously through the winding passages.

Tom led the way down slopes and picked his way up treacherous pathways. His eyes ached from peering at the map. Finally, the group reached a fork in the rocky tunnel – and the red line on the parchment faded.

"We must be close to the royal city," said Tom. "But how do we get out?"

Elenna checked the map and frowned. "Looks as though we'll have to find our own way from here."

Tom looked at the passage to his

left. "I think there's been a rockfall," he whispered. "Perhaps there was an exit there once – but now it's completely sealed."

Another rumble sounded through the ancient stone. Tom tried to stop the panic rising up inside him. But he had to tell Elenna what he was thinking.

"There's no way out," he said, turning to his friend. "We're trapped!"

CHAPTER FOUR
TALES OF THE PAST

"Tom," whispered Elenna, her eyes dark with fear. "If these caves fill with lava, we won't stand a chance. We'll all die!"

Tom swallowed hard. "I know."

"What's wrong?" a woman called nervously.

"Nothing," he said, not wanting the villagers to panic. "I'll just scout ahead. Wait here."

But he had barely walked more than a few steps when he froze. A chill of fear ran through him.

He could hear a scraping, scrabbling noise from the pile of rocks in front of them. Something was trying to break through!

"Epos?" Elenna hissed.

Tom gripped his sword, ready for action. "We'll soon find out!"

Then, to Tom's surprise, Silver leapt forwards and jumped up at the rocks. He was yelping and whining eagerly. Tom placed his ear against the rock – and felt relief flood his whole body.

"We're here!" he shouted, beating the hilt of his sword on the wall. "Can you hear me?"

"What are you doing?" Elenna cried, as a hubbub started up among the villagers.

"I heard voices," he explained.
"There are people outside. A rescue
party!"

Dust showered down on Silver
as a huge rock was heaved away.
Weak sunlight stole into the dark
cave, and a man wearing a helmet
stuck his head through the hole.
Tom recognised the crest on the

helmet at once.

"It's one of King Hugo's soldiers!" he cried.

"We have some survivors, men," the soldier shouted over his shoulder, then he turned back and looked at the filthy-looking people. "I'm here to rescue the villagers from the volcano. Everyone out, quickly – there could be another rockfall at any moment."

Tom stepped aside and watched the villagers as they scrambled out into the daylight. As the soldiers helped them through, he felt a rush of pride. He'd saved them!

"Well done, Tom," said Elenna, smiling as Silver played with the three dogs in the wet grass outside. Storm blew softly against her shoulder. "But now I suppose we should head back to the volcano."

Owen heard them as he walked

towards the cave's exit. "You're going to try and find that magic bird, aren't you?" he whispered.

Tom frowned. "You know about Epos?"

"I...I saw her, a couple of weeks ago." Owen gulped. "She was the most terrifying thing I've ever seen, but no one believed me..."

Elenna put a comforting hand on his shoulder.

"I was lost in the caves," Owen went on. "I think I found her nest. That's where I found your father's armour. She flew right at me, but I ducked and then she just disappeared from the caves. I was lucky."

"Where was this nest?" asked Tom.

"I'm not sure," Owen admitted. "I left chalk arrows on the walls to mark where I'd been. But I didn't see any of them on our way here."

"Well, it seems that Epos has a new nest now – in the volcano," Elenna pointed out. "And it could erupt at any moment!"

"Well, good luck," said Owen, climbing up to the surface. "And be careful!"

Suddenly the king's soldier leapt down into the cave. "What are you two doing?" he asked, peering closely at Tom.

"We have unfinished business in the village," Tom said.

The soldier stared again at Tom's face. "Have I met you before?"

"No, sir," said Tom.

"You remind me of someone I once knew." The soldier nodded. "His name was Taladon. A lad with a taste for danger – just like you!"

Elenna gasped, and Tom's eyes

widened. "I've heard of Taladon," he said, not wanting to give too much away. "How do you know him?"

The soldier shrugged. "It was many years ago, when King Hugo was new to the throne. He recruited some boy knights – and Taladon was one of them."

"He was a knight?" Tom asked, his heart beating fast. "What happened to him?"

The soldier's face fell. "I don't know," he said. He shook Tom's hand and smiled. Then he scrambled back outside.

Tom felt proud and excited. "He knew my father!" His hand tightened round the hilt of his sword. "And my father was a knight! This is my destiny, Elenna. While there's blood in my veins, I will finish the Beast Quest!"

CHAPTER FIVE

THE PLACE OF BATTLE

Tom and Elenna carefully retraced their steps through the caves and winding tunnels. Silver went ahead, his tail wagging as he followed the scent back to the village.

"I'm glad we've got him to guide us," said Elenna, peering round in the candlelight. "I don't recognise any of this."

"Me neither," Tom admitted, leading Storm by his halter. "Hey, what's that?"

Elenna held up her candle to the tunnel wall. A chalk cross had been scratched beside an opening in the rock.

"Owen must have left this to mark his way when he got lost," Tom said. "We could be close to Epos's nest!"

Storm was too large to fit through the gap in the wall. Leaving him to wait in the tunnel, Tom went to see what was on the other side of the crevice. Elenna and Silver followed him.

They found themselves in a larger cave. By the flickering light of their candles, Tom saw sticks, stones and dead leaves bundled together in a large, sprawling mess.

"This is definitely a nest," he

murmured. Then he saw pieces of silver gleaming in the leaves. With shaking hands, he picked out foot armour and a gauntlet. The initial T was scratched into each of them.

"Are those your father's?" Elenna whispered.

Tom nodded. All his life he had

longed to know more about his father. Now he felt that his own fate was linked in some strange way to what had happened to him. He put on the foot armour, and pulled the chainmail gauntlet onto his right hand. They fitted perfectly.

"Come on, let's get back to Storm," said Elenna.

"There's no time to waste," said Tom grimly. "We've got to stop Epos before the volcano blows wide open!"

Feeling somehow stronger in his father's armour, Tom followed Elenna and Silver back out through the gap in the wall to where Storm was waiting patiently in the dark tunnel. Silver led the way out.

As they emerged from the caves, Tom's heart sank.

The skies were unnaturally dark, as if a terrible storm was about to break. The entire forest seemed ablaze, the treetops lost in a huge cloud of black smoke. A bubbling river of red-hot lava snaked around the base of the volcano, like a moat around a castle.

Tom jumped onto Storm's back and

pulled Elenna up behind him. "Come on," he said. "Let's get to the volcano. If I can find Epos and make her angry enough, she'll attack... Then I might just be able to catch her off-guard and cut free that enchanted band."

He pressed his heels to Storm's sides and the stallion leapt forwards, galloping through a copse of trees and onto the main road to the volcano. Silver had to sprint to keep up, with Elenna calling to him, urging him on.

It became hotter and hotter the closer they got to the volcano. The ground shuddered and soon Storm was kicking up ash. The air shimmered with fierce heat. After a while Tom eased Storm to a halt. The stallion hung his head, breathing heavily, his neck and shoulders soaked with sweat.

"Look!" Elenna pointed up at
a dark figure gliding round the
volcano's summit. "There's Epos!"

Tom felt a thrill of fear and wonder
at the sight of the Beast. Its body
glowed with a dark, magical light. As
he watched, Epos plunged down into
the volcano – only to burst back out
seconds later in a torrent of flames
and boiling lava. The lava seared
a path down the side of the volcano,
slowly pooling into the bubbling
moat at ground level.

"If Epos keeps stoking the volcano
like that, the eruption will be
incredible," said Tom. "The lava could
even spread as far as the royal city."

Elenna looked pale. "King Hugo
could end up buried in his own
palace!"

"It would leave the whole kingdom

in chaos," Tom realised. "Exactly what Malvel wants..."

"Tom, look!" shouted Elenna, pointing into the sky. "I think Epos has spotted us!"

Tom felt fear stab at his heart as the flame bird's screech tore through the smoky air. Her red eyes shining, Epos was swooping down to attack!

CHAPTER SIX

THE MOAT OF FIRE

Tom leapt down from Storm, swung his shield from his shoulder and drew his sword, as the shadow of the Beast fell over them. With a battle cry, he lunged upwards with his sword. If he could just cut through the enchanted band…

But Epos's deadly talons knocked the blade from his hand and sent it flying through the air.

Storm reared up and kicked the air as the flame bird swept overhead, sparks of fire peppering the air in her wake. Silver barked ferociously, baring his teeth.

In panic, Tom looked around for his sword. It must have fallen in the

bushes behind him. He would never find it in time to defend another attack!

But then he saw what Elenna was doing. She had climbed down from Storm and was fitting an arrow to her bow. Now she raised her weapon and took careful aim.

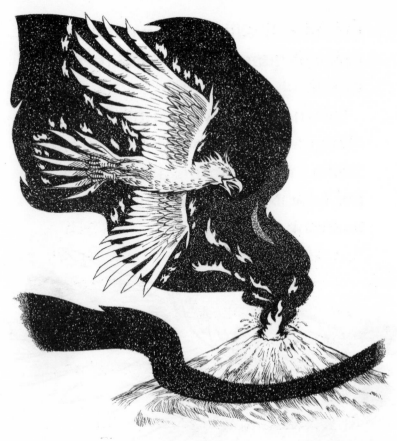

Whoosh! As Epos swooped down, Elenna shot an arrow. The Beast screeched and turned nimbly to avoid it. Quickly Elenna sent another arrow after the first. It whistled past the creature's head. The Beast's eyes burned crimson with rage...then she turned and soared away, spiralling up through the smoke towards the mouth of the volcano.

"Elenna, you did it!" Tom yelled. "You drove her away!"

Silver barked behind them. He had pulled out Tom's sword from the bushes with his teeth. Tom patted the wolf and picked up his weapon.

"How are we ever going to cross that lava to climb the volcano?" Elenna wondered.

"We're not," said Tom. "But *I* am."

She frowned. "Alone?"

He picked up his shield. "This protects me from fire – and after the battle with Tagus the horse-man, it can also help me reach amazing speeds. I can use it as a raft and skim across the surface of the lava."

Elenna's frown deepened. "But Tom, if you fall in—"

"There's no other way," Tom insisted. "And there's no room to take anyone else. I'll stand my best chance of defeating Epos in the heart of her territory, at the top of the volcano. But she might try to attack me as I climb. If she does, I'll need you to drive her off again with those arrows."

"I won't let you down." Elenna's eyes narrowed with determination.

Fear, excitement and anticipation were all jumbled up inside Tom. But he knew one thing for sure – the greatest trial of his life was approaching.

He hugged Elenna. Storm pushed Tom's arm with his nose, then blew gently on his hair. Tom smiled and stroked his horse's neck. Then he crouched down to say goodbye to Silver. The sleek grey wolf licked his hand and gazed up at him intently.

Tom looked at his friends with a mixture of pride and sorrow. They had all grown so close on their Quest. But now he had to leave them. He turned away and walked down the hillside to the lava's edge. His heart was pounding and his skin prickled with the heat, as he carefully slid his shield onto the surface of the molten moat. The enchanted wood hissed and steamed.

"Here goes," said Tom, holding his breath as he stepped lightly onto the shield. It wobbled, but held firm beneath him. Then he dug his sword against the bank and pushed with all his might, propelling himself across the moat of lava.

White-hot drops of lava spat up from the seething lake of fire, and Tom held his arms out to help him balance as his shield skated across the

71

surface, picking up speed as it went.
The talismans given to him by Tagus
and Ferno were both helping him to
cross the deadly moat!

As Tom reached the other side, he
jumped for solid ground with
a whoop of joy. He had made it!

He heard Elenna cheering, and

waved to her. But as he used his sword to fish his smoking shield out of the lava, the ground shook beneath his feet. He looked up to find Epos still circling through the fire-clouds that belched from the top of the volcano.

Up there, his destiny was waiting.

Tom slung the shield over his shoulder, slipped his sword into its scabbard and started to climb.

CHAPTER SEVEN

THE DARK FIGURE

Tom scaled huge crags of rock,
making his way towards the summit
of the volcano. But the ground grew
more and more treacherous. Several
times he slipped on loose stones and
almost fell.

He was clinging to a sheer rockface
when Epos caught sight of him
through the black clouds. With
a piercing shriek, the flame bird

swooped down to attack.

Tom went for his shield. But Epos
grabbed hold of it with her beak and
wrenched it out of Tom's grip.

"No!" Tom shouted, panic-stricken.
He yanked his sword from his
scabbard and swung wildly at Epos.
The Beast retreated a little way, still

holding the shield in her beak, just out of Tom's reach. Then she turned and flew away, fire streaming in her wake.

Tom felt sick as he wiped sweat from his brow. He had lost his best defence – his magical shield. But he had come too far to turn back now.

He continued his steep climb.

Stinking smoke gushed from vents in the trembling rock, stinging his eyes. His throat and lungs burned every time he breathed in, and the fumes made him light-headed. Tom stopped for a moment and drank thirstily from his water bottle. Battling Epos on this terrain wasn't going to be as easy as he thought – if he didn't stumble off the path in all this smoke and fall to his doom first...

"Turn back, Tom. This Quest is beyond you now."

The icy whisper came from behind him. Tom whirled round in fright.

A tall figure in dark robes was standing just a few paces away, wreathed in sickly yellow smoke. Its face was hidden by a hood. Its thin arms were folded across its chest. The figure made Tom shiver, despite the fierce heat.

"Who...who are you?" Tom stammered.

"You know who I am." The figure took a step towards him.

"I am Malvel." Tom felt a dizzying rush of terror. The Dark Wizard, who had enslaved all the Beasts of Avantia for his own evil purpose, was standing before him! With trembling hands, Tom pulled out his sword again.

Malvel laughed. "I know you're brave, Tom, but I didn't think you were stupid. Do you really think a sword can harm me?"

"Stay back," said Tom, trying to stop his voice from shaking.

"You and Aduro are both fools," rasped the dark, hooded figure. "While he has been watching you trek through the kingdom freeing the Beasts, he's been too distracted to hunt for me – and Epos, the most powerful Beast in Avantia." Malvel strode away through the smoke. "You have served me well, boy. Just like your father…"

Tom felt a shiver run through him. "You don't know my father. You're lying."

"Taladon helped me a great deal," said Malvel. "My plans could not have succeeded without him."

"Liar!" Tom bellowed. He raised his sword and angrily flung himself at the hooded figure.

With a laugh of triumph, Malvel disappeared.

Tom found himself hurtling into

empty space. He had run off the edge of a cliff!

Awful truths flashed through his mind as he plummeted through the smoky air. "I let Malvel trick me!" he thought in despair. "He led me off the safe path. He knew that if he made me angry enough, I'd make a mistake."

A fatal mistake.

His Quest was over. He had failed.

He screwed up his eyes as the ground came rushing to meet him.

CHAPTER EIGHT

THE WILL TO SURVIVE

Suddenly Tom's bones jerked as he was yanked back up into the air. A breeze whistled past his ears and his brain spun with confusion. What was happening?

He opened his eyes and gasped. He was dangling helplessly from the talons of Epos! The flame bird had snatched him out of the air and saved his life!

But as the Beast flew upwards through the smoke and clouds, Tom knew with a sinking heart that there could only be one reason for this: Epos had saved him so that she could end his life herself...

No other Beast had shown such spite. How could he hope to triumph over such a deadly enemy?

"No!" thought Tom fiercely. "I won't let my Quest end this way." He hadn't set free the first five Beasts only to be beaten by the last! He thought of the way Malvel had tricked and almost killed him – and an angry determination built up inside him. He would fight Malvel and his evil plans to his last breath. Tom was still clutching his sword, and now he gripped it more tightly than ever.

"While there's blood in my veins," he gasped, "I'll keep fighting!"

Ignoring the pain in his shoulders, Tom reached up and sliced at the golden band. But he couldn't quite reach it. He stretched and strained, but it was no use.

Epos took Tom to the summit of the volcano and spiralled lazily over its gaping mouth. Through the stinging, choking smoke Tom could see an angry, churning sea of white-hot magma, burning up from the depths of the earth. The heat was incredible. It felt strong enough to strip the skin from his bones. The Beast screeched. Tom sensed it was toying with him, enjoying his fear.

Once more he reached up to cut the golden band – just as Epos changed direction. The sword slipped from his grip and tumbled down into the volcano.

"No!" yelled Tom. He felt numb. He had lost his shield *and* his sword. How could he ever win now?

"I've still got my wits," he thought bravely. "I'm not giving up!" he yelled at Epos.

Before the Beast could drop him into the fiery crater, Tom twisted round and grabbed hold of its leg. It was like holding a burning log. Tom shouted in

pain but he couldn't stop now.

Epos gave a bellow of rage and
tried to shake Tom free. The lava
bubbled greedily below them.

"I won't let go!" Tom shouted.

But now Epos was flying towards
the volcano's rim. Tom realised she
was planning to break his grip by
smashing him against the rockface! It
loomed closer, closer…

At the last moment, Tom let go of
Epos and twisted through the air. He
seemed to fall for ages – but at last
he landed on a narrow ledge, the

impact jarring through his body as he scrabbled for a handhold. The rock was burning hot and scorched his skin. But, with the last of his strength, he managed to cling on.

Epos was still circling above him, screeching in fury, and Tom knew he didn't have a hope of climbing over the edge of the rim. "I'm trapped," he thought. "An easy target." But then he saw a crack in the rock – a long, smouldering split. Was it wide enough to let him through? His arms and legs ached, and his skin felt so raw that every movement was agony. But somehow Tom started to squeeze through the gap. If he was fast enough, Epos might think he had simply fallen to his death and give up on him.

"All I need is a chance to get my strength back," he told himself, "to work out a plan..."

With a last, exhausting effort, Tom wriggled through the split in the stone and fell a short way out onto another, cooler ledge – outside the volcano and out of the great flame bird's reach.

Tom lay on the shuddering, smoking ground, gasping for breath. He was overlooking a small, rocky plain close to the volcano's summit. He had no weapons and nowhere to take cover. A dark, steep slope towered above him, leading back up to the mouth of the volcano.

Tom realised then that the crack he had squeezed through was part of a thick black split running horizontally across the slope.

A desperate hope flared up inside him. Above that split were balanced thousands of tons of rock – which seemed to be leaning back into the volcano. If only there was some way of bringing it crashing down, it might plug the fiery heart of the volcano – and ruin Malvel's plans…

"You are too late, boy," came an icy whisper. "Your Quest ends here."

Tom spun round to find the sinister, hooded figure of Malvel had reappeared on the plain in front of him.

Then Epos came swooping down from the rim of the volcano. Tom saw two red eyes glaring down at him. The Beast's giant beak snapped open. Her dark, glowing wings unfolded, and her talons glinted in the dim, crimson light.

The flame bird lunged forwards, ready to tear Tom to pieces...

CHAPTER NINE

THE FIRES OF DESTRUCTION

With a grunt of effort, Tom threw himself out of Epos's path. The Beast was going too fast to stop and crashed into the rockface. Tom scrambled back up.

"You can't win, boy!" Malvel shouted.

Tom tried to escape from the ledge. But Epos was too fast. She lashed out

with one wing and caught Tom on the back of the neck. Tom gasped as he was knocked flying through the air. Before he could rise, Epos grabbed him with her enormous beak. Tom shouted out with pain – it was like being gripped in a vice. Then the flame bird flung him to the ground. Every muscle ached. His body burned with bruises.

But still he forced himself back to his feet.

Malvel snarled, "What does it take to make you give up, boy?"

"More than you've got," Tom cried defiantly.

"I have looked into Elenna's mind," hissed Malvel. "She does not believe you can win."

"That's not true!" Tom pictured his friend's brave smile. "Elenna believes in me, and I believe in her."

"You are a fool if you think that!" Malvel said. "And what about the animals you hold so dear? They have already given up on you. The girl's wolf is leading your horse back through the caves to the royal city."

"Storm and Silver would never leave Elenna!" Tom shouted. "They are loyal."

"They are animals!" Malvel hissed. "Like Epos and all the others – mere Beasts."

Tom stared as Epos hovered above him. Even in his fear, he found the giant flame bird a breathtaking sight. "They're more than just animals," he insisted. "They're…legends."

Epos dropped down and placed her huge talons on Tom's chest.

Malvel chuckled. "It seems Epos does not care for your compliments."

Tom cried out in pain as the giant

flame bird began to crush his ribs.

"Look at the great young hero," Malvel sneered. "You are as weak as your father."

"You're not fit to speak of my father," Tom gasped. He wrestled with Epos's claws, trying to weaken the Beast's grip. The pain was incredible, and the world was starting to spin. "I believe in him," he said through gritted teeth, "as I believe in the Beasts' right to be free!"

Epos's grip on Tom grew tighter still. The ground groaned and shook, as the volcano prepared to explode.

"And I believe," Tom croaked, clutching desperately at the Beast's leg, "that it's my destiny...to beat YOU!"

Tom's right hand – the one on which he wore his father's chainmail gauntlet – closed on the golden band around Epos's ankle.

To Tom's amazement, it tore
through the band as if it were wet
paper. He stared at the scraps of gold
in his hand.

Epos let go of Tom and shrieked. It
was a noise like the earth's core
cracking open. She shook violently,

thrashing her wings, then rose up gracefully into the air, released at last.

"No!" bellowed Malvel, backing away. "It is not possible!"

Then Epos flew straight at Malvel, grabbing him with her lethal talons and lifting him up above the volcano.

"This is not the end, Tom!" Malvel screamed. "We shall meet again!"

Epos held the dark, struggling figure a moment longer above the flames exploding from the mouth of the volcano.

Then the Dark Wizard disappeared in a haze of white light, and the Beast's talons were left clutching empty air. Had Malvel's dark magic destroyed him? Or had he somehow transported himself to safety? Tom didn't know.

With a rasping shriek, Epos plunged down inside the volcano. Tom heard the echoes of the shriek hang in the air for a few moments. Then they too were gone.

"I've done it," Tom murmured. His body was burned and bleeding, but he couldn't stop smiling. "Whatever happened to Malvel, his plans have

been defeated – because I've set Epos free!"

Just then the ground bucked beneath him, and a split opened up, belching fire and thick yellow smoke. Tom sat up in sudden terror. This was no time to congratulate himself. The volcano was about to blow. The kingdom of Avantia was still in danger!

Panting for breath, Tom stared at the steep slope of rock shielding him from the fiery forces of the volcano. So many cracks were running across it, and he remembered his desperate plan. If he could topple all that rock, it might just plug the volcano!

Tom yanked off his father's foot armour. Each piece had a pointed end. He placed one against a narrow crack, and grabbed a rock to use as a hammer. He just had to drive the spikes into the cracks to widen the

splits… With luck it might bring the
rockface tumbling down…

Choking on smoke, he struck the
pointed armour again and again. The
cracks started to widen – but the
rockface didn't move. Desperately, Tom
scooped up the other piece of armour
and wedged it into another crack.

"I can do this," he told himself,
swinging his rock hammer again and
again. Tears of frustration welled up
in his eyes. The piece of rock slipped
from his numb fingers.

It was no good. Tom simply wasn't strong enough.

Suddenly, he felt something watching him. He spun round.

Epos, the mighty flame bird, was hovering in the sky above. The Beast's eyes were no longer red. They shone like purest gold.

As Tom stared in amazement, the Beast flew down and crashed into the rock. Again and again, Epos hurled herself at the stone. Huge splits opened up in the rockface as Epos drove her beak into the stone.

"You understand!" Tom cried in amazement. "You saw what I was trying to do, and you're helping me!" He felt torn. He was so grateful for the Beast's help, but it was awful to watch her flinging herself against the rocks, violet sparks flying from her body.

With new hope, Tom grabbed

another lump of stone and used it to drive his crumpled foot armour deeper still inside the cracks. Working together, he and Epos might just succeed...

At last the huge slope of rock began to crumble! Black zigzags were spreading across it.

"Yes!" Tom cried.

With a last, roaring shriek, Epos flung herself into the centre of the rockface. With a grating, grinding noise, it collapsed.

Tom was standing at the edge of the slope, but the giant flame bird had no time to get clear.

"Epos!" Tom yelled as the Beast disappeared beneath the falling rocks and into the mouth of the volcano.

CHAPTER TEN

THE FINAL ANSWERS

Tom was knocked to his knees as the ground rocked beneath him. He covered his ears as huge crashes echoed all around.

Then the tremors died away. Smoke, mixed with dust, rose up into the black sky. For a long, stunned moment, Tom wondered why it was suddenly so much darker. Then he realised that the fierce glow of the molten lava had been buried beneath thousands of tons of rock. The volcano's fierce fires had been put out.

The kingdom was safe at last!

But Epos was dead. The noble Beast had sacrificed herself for the sake of Avantia.

"No!" Tom shouted, scrambling over the fallen rock, trying to find

some way of reaching the flame bird.
But there was no way through.

Tom barely noticed when some of
the swirling smoke began to shine
and sparkle, and a familiar, red-
cloaked shape appeared beside him.
At last he turned.

"Hello, Wizard Aduro," Tom
whispered.

The old man smiled down at him.
"You have done well, Tom. You have
defeated Malvel – and saved the
kingdom."

Tom cast a glance at the village far
below, still standing. The forest fires
had burned themselves out, and each
tree was now a black skeleton. "I still
don't understand how I broke the
band to set Epos free," he admitted,
removing the chainmail gauntlet.
"Surely my father's old armour can't
be that strong?"

Aduro smiled. "You made it strong, Tom. It was your faith in your father and your friends – and your faith in yourself – that allowed you to break the evil charm. Malvel did not understand goodness or loyalty. So his charms had no defence against one who prized those things so highly."

Tom's gaze fell to the ground. "But I couldn't save Epos. She's dead."

"Are you sure?" the old wizard said gently.

A deep rumbling sound rolled around them. Before Tom could react, an enormous ball of light rose up from the sealed volcano. Something stirred inside it – the golden shadow of a bird. Then the ball of light burst apart and, with a mighty squawk, a gigantic, majestic creature appeared.

"Epos!" Tom cried.

"She is a phoenix," Wizard Aduro reminded him. "She must allow herself to die in flames, so that she can rise anew from the ashes."

The Beast circled above them, flapping her golden wings, leaving trails of golden fire in the air.

"Now she has thrown off her old form, all trace of Malvel's evil has died with it," Aduro murmured. "Thanks to you, Tom, she will be free for ever."

"Wait," whispered Tom. "There's something in her mouth…"

Epos opened her beak. A smoking sword and a blackened, wooden shield fell, landing with a clatter at Tom's feet.

"My sword! My shield!" Tom shouted. "Epos brought them back from the volcano!"

With a last, deafening screech, Epos soared up into the heavens. In her wake she left streaks of magical fire that burned away the dark clouds of volcanic smoke and ash hanging over the village.

Tom laughed as he found himself staring up into the clear blue sky of an early morning.

Aduro put a hand on Tom's shoulder. "It is a new dawn for the whole kingdom – thanks to you, Tom."

Just then, something fell from the sky, right into Tom's hand. It was a sharp, glowing talon. Instinctively, Tom knelt to place it in his shield. At once, a golden light shone out from the shield and bathed his skin.

"What...what's happening?" Tom stammered.

"A reborn phoenix can heal all wounds," Aduro explained.

Tom's body filled with warmth. His burns and cuts disappeared. His pain drained away. But then he felt a swirling sensation. The volcano seemed to spin about him.

"Aduro?" Tom called uncertainly. "Where are you?"

"Do not be afraid," the wizard

murmured. "Someone special wishes to see you – and he does not like to be kept waiting…"

Tom felt a jolt go through his body. His senses spun. He felt as if he were flying. Then the air was suddenly fresh and sweet in his lungs. All was quiet. Gingerly, he opened his eyes to find himself in a large, luxurious room, decorated in crimson and gold. He was kneeling on a polished floor of white marble. A man sat in front of him on a magnificent throne.

With a gasp, Tom realised where he was. He was in the royal palace with his sword and shield – on his knees before the king!

"Greetings, Tom," said King Hugo. "Wizard Aduro has brought you directly to me so I can thank you without delay."

Tom gulped, and bowed his head.

"It was my pleasure, Your Majesty!"

"All Avantia owes you a great debt," the king went on. "Ask for anything you desire, and you shall have it."

Tom rose to his feet and bowed. "Please, Your Majesty, all I want is the answer to one question..." He swallowed hard. "What happened to my father?"

"It is time you knew," the king said. "Taladon the Swift was a boy knight. Many years ago he encountered Epos in the caves near the volcano. Epos was under no spell, but she thought your father was an intruder. Your father fought the Beast – and lost. And from that day on, he made it his mission to know all he could about the Beasts. He went to stay with his brother in Errinel, read old books, gathered secret knowledge...and found a wife, of course."

Tom nodded. "My mother."

"Soon after, Taladon began to dream about the Beasts. Strange and awful nightmares which told him that something bad was going to happen. These nightmares did not go away…" King Hugo leaned forwards. "He believed they were a prophecy that would one day come true. So did your mother. And because they both loved you, they wanted to protect the land in which you would grow up."

Tom listened, astounded, as the king went on.

"Your mother's dying wish was that Taladon should go on a Quest to find out more about the Beasts. That he should track them down all over the world, learn their strengths and weaknesses. That way, if they ever did attack, the kingdom would be prepared – and its people could live without fear."

"But, Your Majesty," Tom began nervously, "Malvel said my father helped him."

Wizard Aduro stepped up beside him. "Malvel stole Taladon's journals, filled with hard-won secret knowledge about the Beasts," he explained. "He used that information to gain control over six of them. That is the only way in which your father helped Malvel."

Tom felt a surge of pride in his father's achievements. "Then I have followed in his footsteps!" He looked hopefully at Aduro. "Do you know where he is now?"

"I do not," Aduro admitted. "He has travelled to far lands now, to places even I cannot see."

"One day I'll find him," Tom vowed. "We will meet, I know it. It's my destiny."

Suddenly, there was a clattering noise outside the throne room, and voices raised in surprise.

The king smiled. "Ah! Aduro has conjured some others who wish to greet you."

The doors to the throne room were thrown open – by Elenna!

"Tom!" she yelled.

Before Tom could say a word, Elenna threw herself into his arms, almost knocking him to the floor as she hugged him tight. "Oh, Tom, you did it!"

"*We* did it," he told her. "I could never have done this without you, Storm and Silver. Where are they?"

"It seems they are inside my throne room!" King Hugo exclaimed.

Tom laughed as Storm clopped over and pushed past Aduro, neighing loudly. Silver dashed in and out of the stallion's legs in excitement, then licked Tom all over his face.

"I'm not sure I've ever entertained

a horse and a wolf in my palace before," laughed King Hugo. "But then, we've never had a hero like Tom before, either." He beamed at Elenna and the animals. "Tonight there shall be a mighty feast – with you, Tom and Elenna, as the guests of honour!"

Tom bowed. "We are grateful, Your Majesty," he said.

"I am the grateful one," said King Hugo. "I shall speak to the people now."

As the king crossed to the royal balcony, Tom looked at Aduro. "Is it really all over? Is Malvel gone for ever?"

"Who can tell?" said Aduro. "Malvel was a great sorcerer with the power to travel great distances in the blink of an eye. This Quest may be over, Tom, but others may lie ahead."

A shiver of excitement ran through Tom. "I'll be ready."

"And we'll face them together," said Elenna.

Storm whinnied and Silver barked, as a gigantic cheer shook the palace. King Hugo had walked out onto the balcony to greet the people, and now he was beckoning to Tom and Elenna.

Tom gulped. "We'd better go and face that crowd!"

Tom and Elenna took their place at King Hugo's side. The streets outside were jammed full of jostling people, all of them clapping and cheering. Tom spotted Owen and Raymond smiling in the crowd, and waved to them.

"You're the kingdom's hero, Tom!" said Elenna excitedly. "Your story will be told throughout the land…"

Tom hardly heard her. For a second he thought he glimpsed a dark, hooded figure... He blinked – and when he looked again, there was nothing. Were his eyes playing tricks on him?

"If Malvel returns," Tom thought gravely, "I shall be waiting."

But right now, it was enough to know he had completed his Beast Quest, and that Elenna, Storm and Silver were close beside him.

Tom smiled and held his sword aloft as the crowd cheered. He thought about the six Beasts, who were now free again to guard the kingdom. Just as they always had, since time began.

JOIN TOM ON HIS NEXT BEAST QUEST SOON!

Win an exclusive
Beast Quest T-shirt and goody bag!

Tom has battled many fearsome Beasts and we want to know
which one is your favourite! Send us a drawing or painting of
your favourite Beast and tell us in 30 words why you think
it's the best.

Each month we will select **three** winners to receive
a Beast Quest T-shirt and goody bag!

Send your entry on a postcard to
BEAST QUEST COMPETITION
Orchard Books, 338 Euston Road, London NW1 3BH.

Australian readers should email:
childrens.books@hachette.com.au

New Zealand readers should write to:
Beast Quest Competition, 4 Whetu Place, Mairangi Bay,
Auckland NZ, or email: childrensbooks@hachette.co.nz

**Don't forget to include your name and address.
Only one entry per child.**

Good luck!

Fight the Beasts,
Fear the Magic

www.beastquest.co.uk

Check out the Beast Quest website for games,
downloads, competitions, animation and all the
latest news about Beast Quest!

Look carefully at the collector cards that you
received free with this book. Do the cards have
a secret code on the back? If they do, you can use this
code to access special secret rooms on the Beast Quest
website. If your cards do not have codes, try again
next time – there are twelve cards to collect and
you get two free with every Beast Quest book!

DON'T MISS

the next set of Beast Quest books. Sign up to the
newsletter on the Beast Quest website so that you will
be the first to know when the new series is released!

by Adam Blade

All priced at £4.99

The Beast Quest books are available from all good
bookshops, or can be ordered direct from the publisher:
Orchard Books, PO BOX 29, Douglas IM99 1BQ.
Credit card orders please telephone 01624 836000
or fax 01624 837033 or visit our website:
www.orchardbooks.co.uk
or e-mail: bookshop@enterprise.net for details.

To order please quote title, author
and ISBN and your full name and address.
Cheques and postal orders should be made payable to
'Bookpost plc.'
Postage and packing is FREE within the UK
(overseas customers should add £2.00 per book).

Prices and availability are subject to change.